DUDDLE PUCK
THE PUDDLE DUCK

BY KARMA WILSON
ILLUSTRATED BY MARCELLUS HALL

MARGARET K. McELDERRY BOOKS • NewYork London Toronto Sydney New Delhi

MARGARET K. McELDERRY BOOKS

An imprint of Simon & Schuster Children's Publishing Division • 1230 Avenue of the Americas, New York, New York 10020 • Text copyright © 2015 by Karma Wilson • Illustrations copyright © 2015 by Marcellus Hall • All rights reserved, including the right of reproduction in whole or in part in any form. • MARGARET K. McELDERRY BOOKS is a trademark of Simon & Schuster, Inc. • For information about special discounts for bulk purchases, please contact Simon & Schuster Special Sales at 1-866-506-1949 or business@simonandschuster.com. • The Simon & Schuster Speakers Bureau can bring authors to your live event. For more information or to book an event, contact the Simon & Schuster Speakers Bureau at 1-866-248-3049 or visit our website at www.simonspeakers.com. • Book design by Sonia Chaghatzbanian • The text for this book is set in Gill Sans. • The illustrations for this book are rendered in watercolor. • Manufactured in China • 0615 SCP • 10 9 8 7 6 5 4 3 2 1 • Library of Congress Cataloging-in-Publication Data • Wilson, Karma. • Duddle Puck the puddle duck / by Karma Wilson, the New York Times bestselling author ; illustrated by Marcellus Hall. — First edition. • pages cm • Summary: A very odd duck that refuses to quack shocks and flusters animals all over the farm with his clucking, honking, oinking, and neighing. • ISBN 978-1-4424-4927-5 (hardcover : alk. paper) — ISBN 978-1-4424-4928-2 (ebook) • [1. Stories in rhyme. 2. Animal sounds—Fiction. 3. Individuality—Fiction. 4. Ducks—Fiction. 5. Domestic animals—Fiction. 6. Humorous stories.] I. Hall, Marcellus, illustrator. II. Title. • PZ8.3.W6976Dud 2015 • [E]—dc23 • 2014032659

FIRST EDITION

To Justin C., who helps me find my own way of saying things
and is a very fine feathered friend. Quack!
—K.W.

To Patra
—M. H.

Silly Duddle Puck
was a funny puddle duck.
All the critters said he was a very odd duck.

He never, ever quacked,
but he often liked to cluck.
Duddle Puck, what a
silly puddle duck.

"Duddle," Henny squawked,
"ducks should always quack!
A proper puddle duck should
really know how to act!"

Duddle only giggled and
threw his head back.
He honked, but he
never, ever quacked.

Gilly Goose waddled by,
and she looked a little shocked.
She honked, "My dearest Duddle,
that is not how ducks should talk."

She flapped her wings indignantly,
and feathers fluttered loose.
"Remember you're a duck,
you're **NOT** a noble goose!"

But Duddle only smiled, and he did a little jig
over to the wallow, where he spied a spotted pig.

"Oink oink," said Duddle.

But the pig just sputtered back,
"Ducks should never oink,
they really ought to quack."

But Duddle didn't quack, as a proper duck should say.

Instead he wandered to the barn and bellowed out a . . .

Hank the Horse was stunned;
he was taken quite aback.

"Ducks should never neigh,
they really oughta quack!"

Duddle danced and sang, "Cluck, honk, oink, neigh!" And everyone was shocked when he added,

HIP-

Gilly Goose was flustered,
and she fussed, "It's just our luck!
This bird-brain doesn't know
that he's actually a duck!"

OINK
CLUCK
HONK
NEIGH
HIP-HIP
HOORAY!

Henny called a meeting for the critters on the farm.

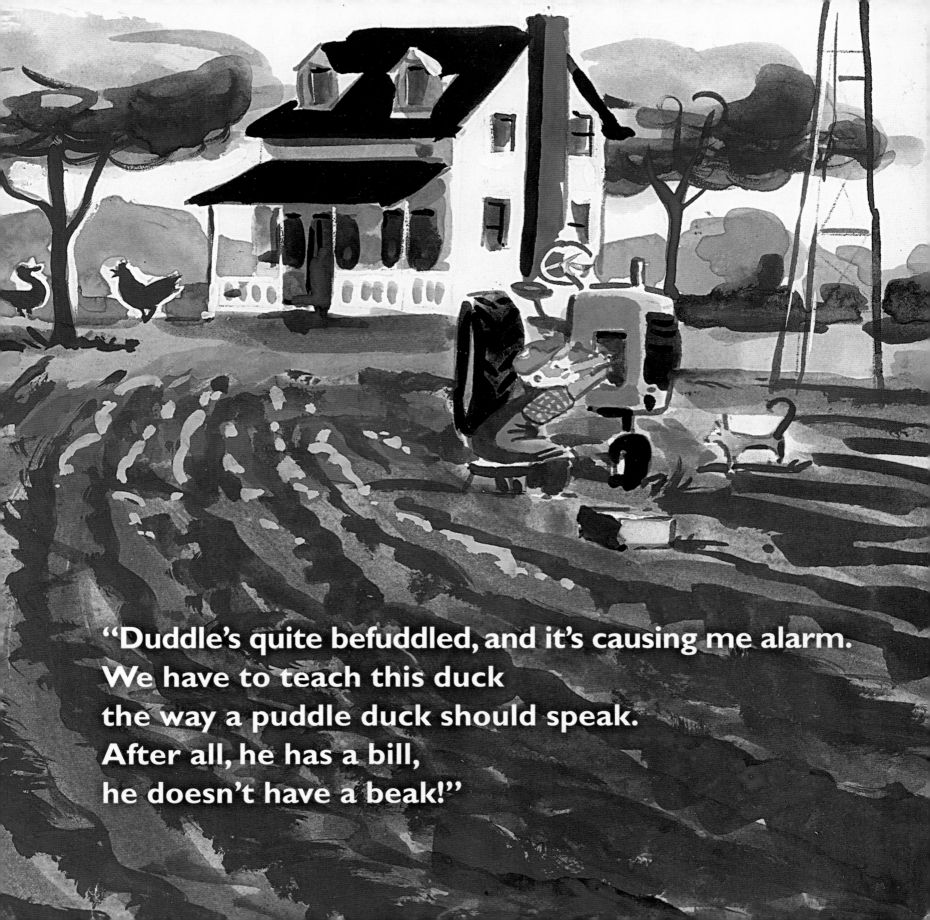

"Duddle's quite befuddled, and it's causing me alarm.
We have to teach this duck
the way a puddle duck should speak.
After all, he has a bill,
he doesn't have a beak!"

The animals lined up and hollered,
"Duddle, please come here!"

They all together spoke out very slow, and very clear.

"This is how a duck should sound;
you've gotten way off track."

Then each and every critter
quacked and quacked.

Duddle winked and smiled.
"Yes, it is true, I am a duck,
and at times I like to moo, or oink,
or maybe even cluck.
But not one of you is a duck."

Then Duddle giggled out with glee.

"And yet you all sound JUST like ducks to me!"

Duddle tipped his head and said,
"I'll do this just for you. . . ."

Then he roared a mighty

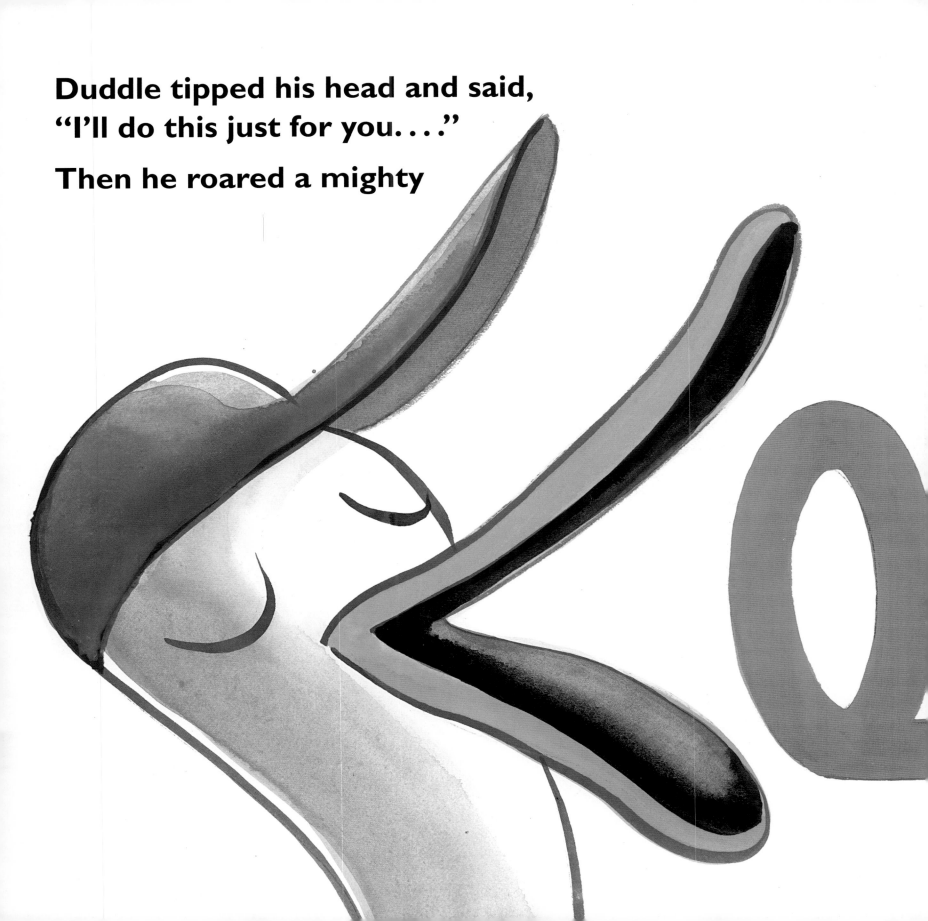

UACK-